MW0074439б

Read to Grow, INC.

providing books for children...

This book is a gift from

Read to Grow

__www.readtogrow.org__

203-488-6800

through the generosity of the

ALCOA
FOUNDATION

Rabbit's Bedtime

Written and Illustrated by Nancy Elizabeth Wallace

Houghton Mifflin Company

Boston

For my wonderful mom, Alexine Wallace,
with so much love
—N.E.W.

The text of this book is set in 22-point Goudy.
The illustrations for *Rabbit's Bedtime* were created using scissors,
a glue stick, tape, tweezers, and origami and found paper.

Library of Congress Cataloging-in-Publication Data

Wallace, Nancy Elizabeth.
Rabbit's bedtime / Nancy Elizabeth Wallace.
p.   cm.
Summary: At bedtime a rabbit ponders the good things that happened during the day
and how there was time to work, time to play, time to dance, laugh, and cuddle.
ISBN 0-395-98266-9
[1. Bedtime — Fiction. 2. Rabbits — Fiction. 3. Stories in rhyme.] I. Title.
PZ8.3.W1585Rab 1999
[E] — dc21   98-53994   CIP   AC

Manufactured in Malaysia
TWP 10 9 8 7 6 5

Bedtime.

What was good about today?

There was . . .

time to work

and time to play.

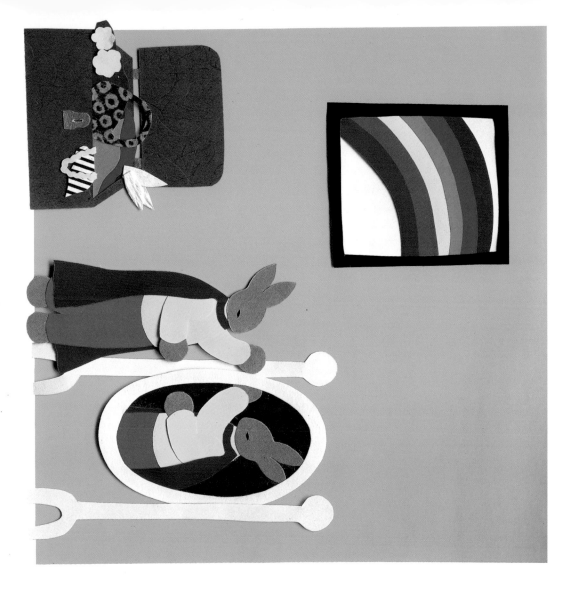

Time to dance

and time to sing.

Time to make a special thing.

Time to laugh and time to giggle.

Time to watch an inchworm wiggle.

Time with others.

Time alone.

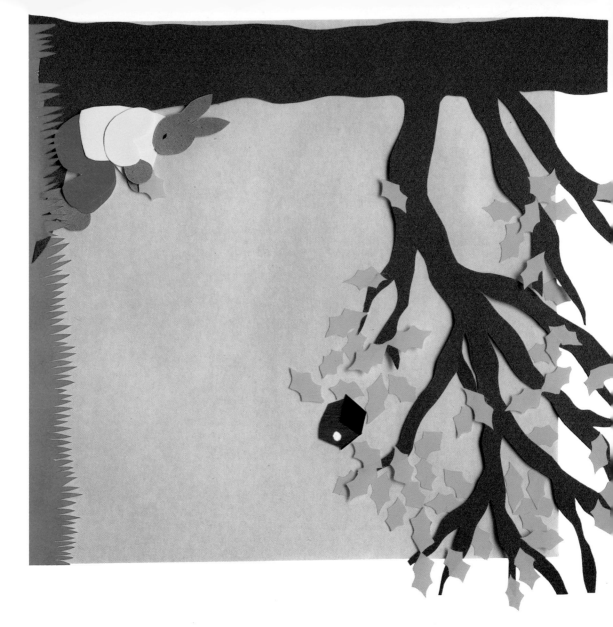

Time to nurture seeds I've sown.

Time to look as a bird soars by.

Time to wonder, how does it fly?

Time to cuddle and feel close and snug.

Time to give and get a hug.

What was good about today?

A lot of things, I would say.

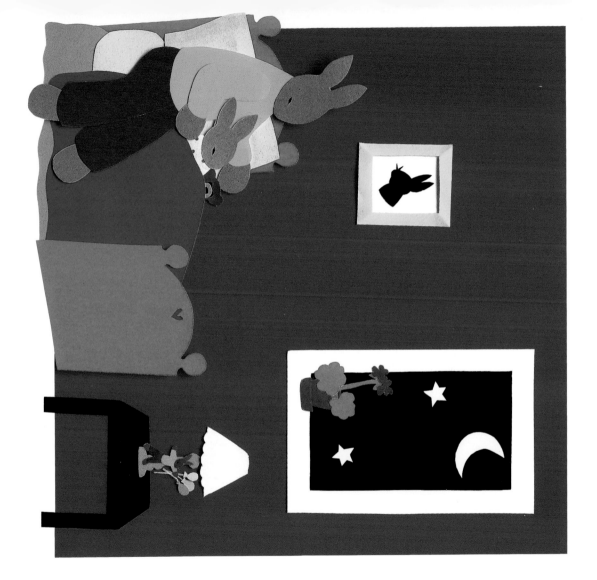

Thank you.